Weekly Reader Children's Book Club Presents

Bear and Mrs. Duck

ELIZABETH WINTHROP

ILLUSTRATED BY
PATIENCE BREWSTER

HOLIDAY HOUSE/NEW YORK

To Priscilla and Hilary, the Mrs. Ducks
in our lives

E.W.

To Heather ("Queen of Sheba"; Restorer
of Spirits) Sargent, for her laughter

P.B.

This book is a presentation of Atlas Editions, Inc.
For information about Atlas Editions book
clubs for children write to:

Atlas Editions, Inc.
4343 Equity Drive
Columbus, Ohio 43228.

Published by arrangement with Holiday House.

Weekly Reader is a federally registered
trademark of Weekly Reader Corporation.

Library of Congress Cataloging-in-Publication Data

Winthrop, Elizabeth.
Bear and Mrs. Duck.

Summary: Once he overcomes his initial fear, Bear has
fun playing with his new baby sitter, Mrs. Duck.
[1. Baby sitters—Fiction. 2. Bears—Fiction.
3. Ducks—Fiction.] I. Brewster, Patience, Ill.
II. Title.
PZ7.W768Bd   1988   [E]   87-25129
ISBN 0-8234-0687-3
1998 edition

Bear and Mrs. Duck

Nora loved Bear. They ate lunch together. They read stories together. They slept in beds right next to each other.

One day, Nora had to go to the store. Bear was sick with a cold. He had to stay inside.

"Bear," said Nora. "This is Mrs. Duck. She'll take good care of you while I'm gone."

Bear looked at Mrs. Duck. He did not like her funny floppy feet. He did not like her beady black eyes. He did not like her fat fluffy tail.

Bear ran to Nora. Nora gave him a kiss. "Be good, Bear," she said.

"Don't go, Nora," cried Bear, and he burst into tears.

"I'll be home soon," said Nora. "I love you very much." Nora gave Bear a big fat hug and an extra squeeze.

"Good-bye," she called as she went out the door.

"I'm going to sit and wait for Nora to come home," said Bear to Mrs. Duck.

"Would you like to draw a picture while you wait?" Mrs. Duck asked.

"No!" cried Bear.

"Would you like to read a book?" Mrs. Duck asked.

"I miss Nora," said Bear.

"Of course you do. But she'll be back soon," said Mrs. Duck.

"I'm going to sit here and wait," said Bear.

So Bear waited. He stared at the ceiling. He kicked his covers off. He pulled them back on.

"Waiting is very boring," said Bear.

"Yes it is," said Mrs. Duck. "Shall we draw a picture while you wait?"

"We don't have any crayons," said Bear. He was not going to show Mrs. Duck the crayons in the box under his bed. The toys in that box were his favorite toys. He only showed them to Nora.

"Look, I brought some with me," said Mrs. Duck.

The crayons were big and fat and brightly colored. Bear wanted to hold the blue one. Blue was his favorite color.

"All right," he said. "But I am still waiting."

Bear drew a picture of Nora. He colored Nora's dress blue. Mrs. Duck colored Nora's hair brown.

"That looks just like Nora," said Mrs. Duck. "You draw very well, Bear."

"Thank you," said Bear. "But I am still waiting."

"Yes, you are," said Mrs. Duck. "Would you like to read a story next?"

"The books are too high up," said Bear. "Nora always gets them down for me."

"Which is your favorite book?" asked Mrs. Duck.

"The blue one on the very top," said Bear. "It's the one about three bears on a picnic."

Mrs. Duck flapped to the top shelf. She picked out Bear's favorite book and floated down again.

"Wow," said Bear. "That was easy."

Mrs. Duck read Bear the story. Bear snuggled up next to her. Her white feathers felt soft and smooth.

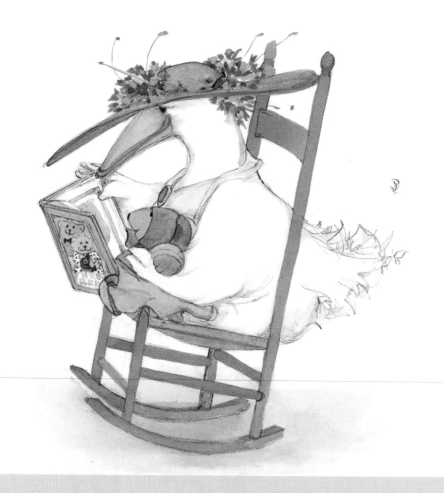

"What shall we do now?" asked Bear.

"We could wait some more," said Mrs. Duck.

"But waiting is SO boring," said Bear. "Let's roll a ball back and forth."

"I forgot to bring a ball with me," said Mrs. Duck.

"I have one," said Bear.

He pulled the box out from under his bed.
There on top of his books and his crayons and his
toy boats sat his big blue ball.

He rolled it to Mrs. Duck. She rolled it back. Bear giggled. "You look funny upside down," he said.

They played ball until Bear got bored. "Will Nora be home soon?" Bear asked.

Mrs. Duck looked at the clock. "Very soon," she said. "Do you want to play hide-and-go-seek?" she asked.

"Yes," cried Bear. "That's my favorite game. Nora says I am very good at it."

Bear hid his eyes and waited as long as he could. "Ready or not, here I come," he called.

He looked under the bed.

He looked behind
the shower curtain.

He peeked into the closet.

"Mrs. Duck, you are a very good hider," he
shouted.

"Come and get me," she called back.

He followed her voice into the kitchen. She was sitting on top of a cabinet. "There you are," Bear said. "I found you."

"Yes, you did," said Mrs. Duck. "You have bright eyes, Bear."

When Bear hid, it took Mrs. Duck a long, long time to find him. He was sitting in the bathtub.

"Let's play with my toy boats," Bear said.

Mrs. Duck filled the bathtub with water. Bear dropped all his boats in the sea.

"I can't reach my sailboat," Bear cried. "It's floated too far away."

Mrs. Duck climbed into the bathtub and paddled over to the sailboat. She pushed it back to Bear with her yellow beak.

"You're a good swimmer," Bear said.

"Thank you, Bear," said Mrs. Duck.

"I want to get in too," said Bear.

"Not today," said Mrs. Duck. "You have a cold. Next time I come, you can swim with me."

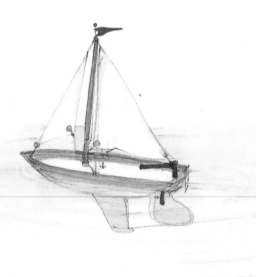

The door opened.

"I'm home," said Nora. "Where are you, Bear?"

"Here I am," Bear cried, and he ran down the hall into Nora's arms.

Nora gave Bear a big fat hug and an extra squeeze.

"I missed you," said Nora.

"I missed you too," Bear said.

Mrs. Duck put on her cape. "Good-bye, Bear. See you soon."

"Good-bye, Mrs. Duck," said Bear.

"Did you have fun with Mrs. Duck?" asked Nora.

"Well," said Bear, "she's not the same as you."

"No, she's not," said Nora.

"But she can fly," said Bear.

"Wow," said Nora.

"And she's a good swimmer," said Bear. "Next time she comes, she says I can swim with her in the bathtub."

"That sounds like fun," said Nora.

"But she's not the same as you," said Bear. And he gave Nora a big fat hug and an extra squeeze.